Sofia the Dreamer and her Magical Afro

With love
Jessica

For my parents who nurtured me and my hair.

TALLAWAH PUBLISHING
www.tallawahpublishing.com

Copyright © Tallawah Publishing 2020
Text and illustrations © Jessica N. Wilson 2020

First published in the UK in 2020 by Tallawah Publishing, London

A catalogue record for this book is available from the British Library.

ISBN 978-1-5272-5909-6

Book Design by Lee-May Lim and Paul Martin of Threeshadesred
Printed in Lithuania

Sofia
the Dreamer
and her
Magical Afro

Written by Jessica Wilson

Illustrated by Tom Rawles

TALLAWAH PUBLISHING

Every Sunday afternoon, Sofia's mum
washes and combs her hair.

When anyone touches her magical afro,
Sofia becomes very sleepy!

Sofia's hair is in two-strand twists,
she grabs her brush and starts to sing!

Looking in the mirror,
she remembers a man
dancing on an album cover.

Sunlight floods Sofia's eyes.
She sees the blue ocean,
palm trees and mountains high.
Beside her is a man whose hair
is long and twisted like vines.

"Yu want a mango, empress?" he asks.
"Yes please," Sofia replies, "I like your hat.
Why do you wear your hair like that?"

"I am a rasta. My hair is a lion's mane.
We believe all people are the same.
We believe in the unity of all living things.
That's why we don't eat meat.
I am a vegetarian."

"Me too!" remarks Sofia, "I love fruit,
especially apples, they are my favourite!"

"Yes little rasta! You overstand!
Not every dread is a rasta,
not every rasta is a dread.
It's what's in your heart,
not what's on your head!"

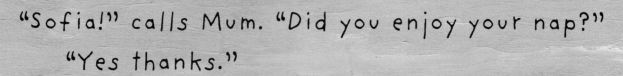

"Sofia!" calls Mum. "Did you enjoy your nap?"
   "Yes thanks."
"And Sofia?"
   "Yes Mum?"
"Where did you find that rasta cap?"

The following Sunday
Mum conditions
Sofia's hair with avocado,
then blow-dries it
into a **GINORMOUS** afro.

'My hair is fluffy like a cloud,'
Sofia thinks. Sofia blinks.

A yellow taxi whizzes by.
The buildings are high
as **GIANTS**.

"Where am I?" Sofia wonders.

"We are in Los Angeles,"
a woman answers.

She is wearing a black leather
jacket with a badge displaying
a picture of a panther.

"Your hair is even **BIGGER**
than mine!" Sofia ponders.

"My hair is a symbol of **POWER**,"
declares the woman, raising her fist.
"I stand for **EQUAL RIGHTS,**
FREEDOM and **JUSTICE**."

"You believe everyone should be
treated with respect?" Sofia says.
The lady nods. Her afro sways.

"What is that shining in your hair?"

"It's my afro pic. Take it as a gift."
Sofia's fingers and the lady's touch.

"It's time for lunch!" shouts Mum.
"Sofia, you nodded off again!"

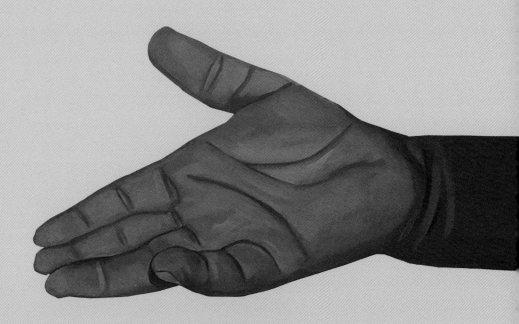

Next Sunday, Mum finishes
Sofia's final canerow braid and slips
a tiny white shell on to the end.

Sofia reaches up to touch but
the scolding sun burns her back.

Ouch!

She is in a field.
Tall tips of plants seek
the brilliant sky.

A knife sweeps! Sofia dives.

"I'm sorry, I didn't
see you there!"

"Our hair is the same!" Sofia exclaims.

"Of course! We have been plaiting
this style since the Stone Age
in a land called Ethiopia."

"Ethiopia? Where's that?"

"The East of Africa.
Now we call them canerows
because they are straight
just like these crops
I must tend and plant.

Knowing your history is important
like sewing seeds, the better
you water, the more you reap."

The grass rustles.

"You must go now!"
hisses the woman.

"Will we meet again?"
asks Sofia.

The woman smiles.

"I will flow through your veins
like a stream,
protect you during the day
and watch over you as you dream
but now, you must go."

Sofia touches the hem of the lady's skirt
and finds her feet are no longer in the dirt
but safe and warm in bed.

This Sunday, Sofia has the flu
and instead of Mum fixing her hair,
Sofia sleeps through the afternoon!
"Achoo!" she sneezes,
"ACHOO! ACHOO!"

Her hair is tangled like a bird's nest.
Mum has put roses on Sofia's desk
to cheer her up whilst she rests.

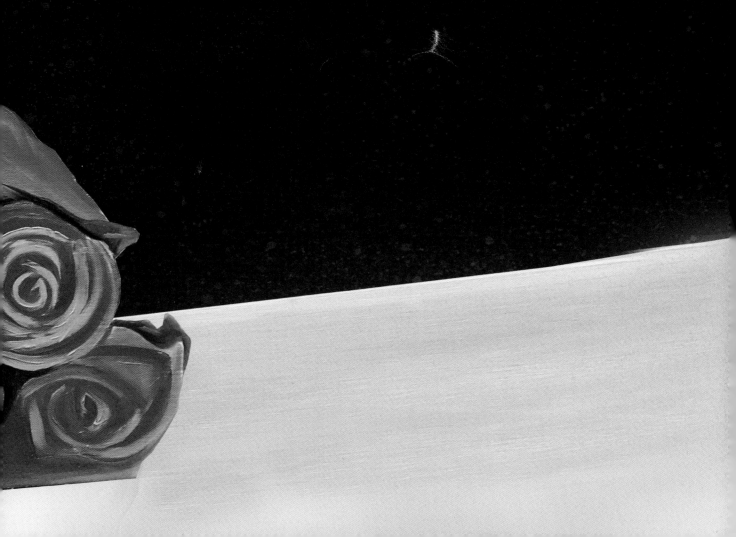

Sofia dozes and floats up
through her open window,
keeps rising
until the world is a dot
and she is hovering by the moon.

She soars past Jupiter and Mars
and looks down
to see a swerve of stars.

Sofia is above the universe!
The galaxy is a spiral,
just like her curls!

Up above, Sofia thinks of her mum
and realises what respect and unity
have in common.

Sofia knows it is **love**.

Love washes your hair
and combs
through the tangles.

Love is joy.
Love empowers.

When you are unwell
love buys you flowers.

Love is a gift
from the ancestors
to their sons and daughters.

Love is respect.
Love is positivity.

Love unites us and sets us free.
Love connects all living beings.

To give and receive love
is the answer to everything.

A special thank-you to Alfred Wilson, Doreen Wilson,
The GoFundMe Team, Kenya McIntyre, Sam Cottman,
Geraldine Cumberbatch, Nadine Onitiri-Coker, Krista Farrell,
Shenel Peart, Paschalis Christou, Maya Sela, Judith Kay,
Patsy Bovell, Bethany West, Aisha Gittens, Yinka Williams,
Kadisha Robertson, Tiph'arah Emeth, Maisy Adams, Sophie
Edmonson, Zach Meier, Kem Clemence, Mary-Jane Kerr,
Hannah Kate Kelly, Nelson Abbey, Samantha Whiteside,
Clive Wilson, Pauline Bailey, Megan Vernon, Paul Martin,
Sharon Martini, Frances Musetti, Rohan Nurse
and Candace Wilson-Nurse.

Jessica Wilson is a writer of Jamaican and British descent.

Jessica was a participant within Penguin Random House's
WriteNow, shortlisted for the 2018 Aesthetica Creative
Writing Award and winner of a GoFundMe award.

Her first poetry collection is entitled 'The bulldog and
the hummingbird'. www.jessica-wilson.com